MAD LIBS JUNIOR™

SCOOBY-DOO!™
MAD LIBS JUNIOR

By Roger Price and Leonard Stern

PSS!
PRICE STERN SLOAN

MAD LIBS JUNIOR™ is a game for kids who don't like games!
It can be played by one, two, three, four, or forty.

RIDICULOUSLY SIMPLE DIRECTIONS:

At the top of each page in this book, you will find four columns of words, each headed by a symbol. Each symbol represents a part of speech. The symbols are:

★	☺	→	?
NOUNS	ADJECTIVES	VERBS	MISC.

MAD LIBS JUNIOR™ is fun to play with friends, but you can also play it by yourself! To begin, look at the story on the page below. When you come to a blank space in the story, look at the symbol that appears underneath. Then find the same symbol on this page and pick a word that appears below the symbol. Put that word in the blank space, and cross out the word, so you don't use it again. Continue doing this throughout the story until you've filled in all the spaces. Finally, read your story aloud and laugh!

EXAMPLE:

"Good-bye!" he said, as he jumped into his _____ and _____
                                                  ★   →

off with his pet _____ .
                        ?

★ NOUNS	☺ ADJECTIVES	→ VERBS	? MISC.
car	curly	drove	hamster
boat	purple	~~danced~~	dog
roller skate	wet	drank	cat
taxicab	tired	twirled	~~giraffe~~
~~surfboard~~	silly	swam	monkey

"Good-bye!" he said, as he jumped into his ___SURFBOARD___ and ___DANCED___
                                                  ★   →

off with his pet ___GIRAFFE___ .
                        ?

In case you haven't learned about the parts of speech yet, here is a quick lesson:

A **NOUN** ★ is the name of a person, place, or thing. *Sidewalk, umbrella, bathtub,* and *roller blades* are nouns.

An **ADJECTIVE** ☺ describes a person, place, or thing. *Lumpy, soft, ugly, messy,* and *short* are adjectives.

A **VERB** ➔ is an action word. *Run, jump,* and *swim* are verbs.

MISC. ? can be any word at all. Some examples of a word that could be miscellaneous are: *nose, monkey, five*, and *blue*.

MAD LIBS JUNIOR™ is fun to play with friends, but you can also play it by yourself! To begin, look at the story on the page below. When you come to a blank space in the story, look at the symbol that appears underneath. Then find the same symbol on this page and pick a word that appears below the symbol. Put that word in the blank space, and cross out the word, so you don't use it again. Continue doing this throughout the story until you've filled in all the spaces. Finally, read your story aloud and laugh!

THE GANG'S ALL HERE!

★ NOUNS	☺ ADJECTIVES	➡ VERBS	? MISC.
sausages	crazy	paddle	oven
teapots	funny	kick	rodeo
goldfish	beautiful	jump	studio
scuba divers	muddy	slam	stable
ponies	handsome	wash	freezer
butterflies	furry	dunk	bathtub
hamburgers	squishy	dribble	boat
hair dryers	bright	throw	school
bathtubs	gloomy	cuddle	closet
kittens	icy	kiss	museum
potatoes	sunny	play	boardwalk
pork chops	jumpy	marry	ocean

MAD LIBS JUNIOR™
THE GANG'S ALL HERE!

The Mystery Inc. gang is so _____! Daphne, with her

_____, red hair and fashionable _____, helps the

gang make important decisions, like when it's time for them to go to the

_____. Then there is Velma, who is the _____ one

of the group. She is great at finding _____ to help the gang

solve mysteries. Fred is considered the leader of the _____.

With his charming, good _____, he is really a/an

_____ detective! Shaggy is a/an _____ member of

Mystery, Inc. Although he always helps the group solve _____

mysteries, he'd much rather _____ with his Great Dane or eat

at his favorite restaurant, the Chunky _____. And who can

forget Scooby! He is always the one to _____ the day!

MAD LIBS JUNIOR™ is fun to play with friends, but you can also play it by yourself! To begin, look at the story on the page below. When you come to a blank space in the story, look at the symbol that appears underneath. Then find the same symbol on this page and pick a word that appears below the symbol. Put that word in the blank space, and cross out the word, so you don't use it again. Continue doing this throughout the story until you've filled in all the spaces. Finally, read your story aloud and laugh!

WHAT'S COOKIN', SCOOBY-DOO?

★ NOUNS	☺ ADJECTIVES	➡ VERBS	? MISC.
elephants	fluffy	bake	airport
lemons	wet	dance	kitchen
turkeys	snowy	wiggle	Dumpster
sardines	crazy	whistle	backyard
peanuts	crunchy	drive	birdcage
hair balls	gross	snowboard	bakery
crackers	tangy	wash	bathtub
liverwurst	steamy	sleep	fountain
mushrooms	crispy	fry	playpen
baseballs	dirty	bathe	gas station
ostriches	foamy	wag	bathroom
bugs	grimy	squash	aquarium

MAD LIBS JUNIOR
WHAT'S COOKIN', SCOOBY-DOO?

Scooby-Doo decided to make dinner for Shaggy and the gang. "Cool,

Scoob," said Shaggy. "Let's _____ ➡ to the _____ **?** and

buy groceries." "What should we _____ ➡, Scoob?" asked Shaggy.

"Ret's rake racos!" cried Scooby. Scooby and Shaggy grabbed

_____ 😊 shredded _____ ★, lettuce and tomatoes,

chopped _____ ★, and chips and _____ ★. When they

got home, Shaggy began to _____ ➡ the _____ ★ while

Scooby set the table. When Velma, Daphne, and Fred walked into the

_____ **?**, they yelled, "Yahoo, tacos! They look _____ 😊!

Thanks, Scooby!" Scooby replied, "Rou're relcome!"

MAD LIBS JUNIOR™ is fun to play with friends, but you can also play it by yourself! To begin, look at the story on the page below. When you come to a blank space in the story, look at the symbol that appears underneath. Then find the same symbol on this page and pick a word that appears below the symbol. Put that word in the blank space, and cross out the word, so you don't use it again. Continue doing this throughout the story until you've filled in all the spaces. Finally, read your story aloud and laugh!

MYSTERY INC.

★	☺	→	?
NOUNS	**ADJECTIVES**	**VERBS**	**MISC.**
bandits	odd	sleep	oceans
mice	fluffy	drive	mansions
zebras	sparkly	mash	parks
pianos	icky	squeak	fields
kites	sleepy	laugh	rodeos
worms	wiggly	rip	arcades
Popsicles	smiley	crush	bookstores
lemons	cutesy	mix	carnivals
pizzas	shiny	paddle	stables
beans	creepy	ride	kitchens
squashes	bright	grin	basements
brussels sprouts	clumsy	dance	pet shops

MAD LIBS JUNIOR.
MYSTERY INC.

Mystery Inc. is one of the most _____ detective teams

around! But did you ever wonder how the _____ Mystery

Inc. gang was formed? It all started with a Great Dane named Scooby-

Doo. He and his owner, Shaggy, met up with three _____

_____ named Fred, Daphne, and Velma. They all had one

thing in common—they loved to _____ mysteries! The

_____ decided to form a/an _____ club and

called it Mystery Inc. Their adventures include visiting haunted

_____, ghost _____, creepy amusement

_____, and even abandoned _____! But no

matter what _____ places they go to, Mystery Inc. always

manages to catch the spooky _____!

MAD LIBS JUNIOR™ is fun to play with friends, but you can also play it by yourself! To begin, look at the story on the page below. When you come to a blank space in the story, look at the symbol that appears underneath. Then find the same symbol on this page and pick a word that appears below the symbol. Put that word in the blank space, and cross out the word, so you don't use it again. Continue doing this throughout the story until you've filled in all the spaces. Finally, read your story aloud and laugh!

A CLUE FOR SCOOBY-DOO, PART I

★ NOUNS	☺ ADJECTIVES	➡ VERBS	? MISC.
socks	fluffy	fry	airport
flippers	spooky	investigate	garage
mushrooms	furry	leap	restaurant
bagels	spiky	scramble	basement
jewels	sugary	tug	shack
fingernails	windy	chomp	arcade
hot dogs	dark	doodle	kitchen
crackers	sparkly	squash	stadium
bugs	rocky	hoot	outhouse
sandwiches	wavy	twist	doghouse
sardines	snowy	crash	taco stand
clams	happy	peek	circus

One day when Mystery Inc. was hanging out at the _____ **?**, they

got a _____ 😊 phone call from the owner of the town art

museum. Somebody had stolen one of their famous _____ ★!

Mystery Inc. needed to figure out a _____ 😊 way to solve the

crime. "The first thing we need to _____ ➡ is evidence," said

Fred. "Let's go to the _____ **?**. Maybe someone left their

_____ ★ or a pair of _____ ★ behind," Fred stated.

"_____ 😊 idea, Fred," said Velma. "We should _____ ➡

over to the _____ **?** now before any time is wasted." As the

gang got ready to _____ ➡, Scooby yawned and said, "Ri ram

rungry!" Shaggy laughed and said, "Scoob, we don't have time to

_____ ➡ Scooby Snacks!"

MAD LIBS JUNIOR™ is fun to play with friends, but you can also play it by yourself! To begin, look at the story on the page below. When you come to a blank space in the story, look at the symbol that appears underneath. Then find the same symbol on this page and pick a word that appears below the symbol. Put that word in the blank space, and cross out the word, so you don't use it again. Continue doing this throughout the story until you've filled in all the spaces. Finally, read your story aloud and laugh!

A CLUE FOR SCOOBY-DOO, PART II

★ NOUNS	☺ ADJECTIVES	➡ VERBS	? MISC.
worms	crazy	dance	bathroom
toys	bubbly	wag	attic
chips	small	jump	park
peanuts	bouncy	scratch	fish tank
books	quiet	pull	concert
raisins	stormy	shimmy	roller rink
hamburgers	shaky	draw	Dumpster
pickles	grouchy	wave	beach
clams	tired	hunt	library
bugs	scary	bark	kitchen
muscles	wormy	fly	barn
mirrors	crunchy	grab	bakery

After the gang got to the _____ **?**, they started to

_____ **➡** for clues. Fred and Daphne began dusting for

_____ **★** while Velma took her magnifying glass and looked for

_____ **★**. That didn't leave much else for Scooby and Shaggy to

do, so they both wandered around the empty _____ **?**.

Suddenly, they heard a _____ 😊 noise! They both looked in

the _____ 😊 _____ **?** and saw a _____ 😊

shadow. "Maybe that's the thief!" yelled Shaggy. Scooby and Shaggy

ran to the _____ **?**, but they were too late to catch the

_____ 😊 shadow. Scooby looked down at the _____ **★**

and pointed. "Rook, Raggy. A rue!" Sure enough, there was a clue left

behind. The mysterious shadow had dropped its watch!

MAD LIBS JUNIOR™ is fun to play with friends, but you can also play it by yourself! To begin, look at the story on the page below. When you come to a blank space in the story, look at the symbol that appears underneath. Then find the same symbol on this page and pick a word that appears below the symbol. Put that word in the blank space, and cross out the word, so you don't use it again. Continue doing this throughout the story until you've filled in all the spaces. Finally, read your story aloud and laugh!

THE MYSTERY MACHINE

★ NOUNS	😊 ADJECTIVES	➡ VERBS	? MISC.
onions	scruffy	sing	bathroom
caterpillars	fluffy	fly	bookstore
sandwiches	small	giggle	café
puppies	muddy	hop	school
earrings	sticky	doodle	jungle
sardines	grubby	nap	castle
burritos	wacky	swim	rodeo
squirrels	tired	flap	garage
tuna	smart	whistle	diner
peanut butter	nutty	stomp	playground
liver	cuddly	juggle	park
cookies	creamy	dance	beach

The Mystery Machine is such a _____ vehicle! It's bright blue

with orange and yellow _____ all over it. The _____

in the van is filled with all sorts of tracking devices and _____

so Mystery Inc. can _____ any mystery that comes their way!

Velma and Daphne love to _____ in the van because they can

blast their favorite _____ on the stereo and _____

along! Sometimes if Fred drives too _____, the van starts to

_____. Rut Ro! Luckily, they always keep a spare tire in the

_____ so they'll always be able to _____ to their

destination safely. But Scooby's favorite thing about the van is the

_____ box of _____ that Shaggy keeps hidden in the

glove compartment!

MAD LIBS JUNIOR™ is fun to play with friends, but you can also play it by yourself! To begin, look at the story on the page below. When you come to a blank space in the story, look at the symbol that appears underneath. Then find the same symbol on this page and pick a word that appears below the symbol. Put that word in the blank space, and cross out the word, so you don't use it again. Continue doing this throughout the story until you've filled in all the spaces. Finally, read your story aloud and laugh!

A SURPRISE FOR SHAGGY

★ NOUNS	☺ ADJECTIVES	→ VERBS	? MISC.
milkshake	awesome	swim	zoo
pizza	gigantic	jump	ranch
toenail	wacky	sing	carnival
burrito	crazy	sleep	circus
toilet	little	boogie	doghouse
boat	giggly	skip	forest
pancake	crusty	slide	arcade
muffin	gooey	bop	parking lot
cupcake	muddy	kick	playground
puppy	soft	shout	bakery
diaper	squishy	cry	igloo
kitten	tasty	wipe	ski lodge

A SURPRISE FOR SHAGGY

Scooby decided that he was going to throw Shaggy a/an _____ 😊

surprise birthday party at the _____ ? . Scooby asked Fred to take

him to the _____ ? so they could buy some _____ 😊

party decorations. Scooby bought balloons, a _____ ★ , and a giant

birthday _____ ★ from Shaggy's favorite _____ ? . After

Scooby and the gang finished decorating for the party, Scooby told Shaggy

to come to the _____ ? because they had a/an _____ 😊

mystery to solve. "Zoinks!" said Shaggy. "I'll be right there!" When Shaggy

arrived at the _____ ? , the gang jumped out and yelled, "Happy

birthday, Shaggy!" Shaggy was so _____ 😊 that he started to

_____ ! ➡

MAD LIBS JUNIOR™ is fun to play with friends, but you can also play it by yourself! To begin, look at the story on the page below. When you come to a blank space in the story, look at the symbol that appears underneath. Then find the same symbol on this page and pick a word that appears below the symbol. Put that word in the blank space, and cross out the word, so you don't use it again. Continue doing this throughout the story until you've filled in all the spaces. Finally, read your story aloud and laugh!

SPORTY SCOOBY

★	😀	➡	?
NOUNS	**ADJECTIVES**	**VERBS**	**MISC.**
meatball	sloppy	toss	museum
frog	awesome	skip	toy store
donut	cheery	bite	hockey rink
toenail	slippery	boogie	birdcage
toilet	giggly	chew	cafeteria
orange	slimy	slam	basement
lasagna	dazzling	swing	fountain
football	great	hit	racetrack
worm	dirty	walk	hospital
egg	gooey	hop	cemetery
elbow	muddy	wash	warehouse
piglet	grumpy	climb	deli

SPORTY SCOOBY

Scooby is a/an _____ athlete! He loves to play all kinds of

_____ sports. One of his favorite things to do with his best

_____ Shaggy is to play a game of catch. Every afternoon after

they've finished solving _____ mysteries, they _____ ➡

in the Mystery Machine and head to their favorite _____ ❓ .

Scooby also likes to play tennis in the _____ ❓ , but Shaggy

prefers to _____ ➡ a football in the _____ ❓ . Luckily,

Velma is a/an _____ tennis player, so she takes Scooby to

the _____ ❓ to play about once a week. If it's _____

outside, Shaggy and Scooby _____ ➡ to the _____ ❓ and

go skating, or they _____ ➡ at home and snack on a/an

_____ ★ .

MAD LIBS JUNIOR™ is fun to play with friends, but you can also play it by yourself! To begin, look at the story on the page below. When you come to a blank space in the story, look at the symbol that appears underneath. Then find the same symbol on this page and pick a word that appears below the symbol. Put that word in the blank space, and cross out the word, so you don't use it again. Continue doing this throughout the story until you've filled in all the spaces. Finally, read your story aloud and laugh!

A CLUE FOR SCOOBY-DOO, PART III

★	☺	→	?
NOUNS	**ADJECTIVES**	**VERBS**	**MISC.**
diapers	squishy	kissed	bedroom
onions	awesome	ran	circus
fish sticks	wacky	leaped	aquarium
ice-cream cones	cool	crept	ballroom
buttons	amazing	squealed	restaurant
daisies	fishy	pulled	Dumpster
doctors	loud	hugged	arcade
roaches	stubby	squeezed	golf course
oysters	salty	smushed	tunnel
waffles	frosty	twisted	farm
flowers	stinky	spooked	airport
muffins	icky	smelled	cafeteria

Shaggy looked closely at the watch. "Zoinks!" he yelled. "Let's go show this

to the rest of the _____!" "Look, _____!" yelled

★   ★

Shaggy. "Scooby found a clue! And look! There are _____

★

printed on the back! What do you think they mean?" "I don't know,

Shaggy," admitted Fred. Suddenly, Velma exclaimed, "Let's show this to

the _____ owner. Maybe he'll know!" The owner

?

_____ and said, "_____ job! Let's have a look!"

➡   ☺

Then he said, "Wait a minute. My _____ friend has the same

☺

exact watch." Daphne gasped. "Do you think he was the one who

_____ the museum?" "I don't know," admitted the museum

➡

owner. "But let's go to his _____ and find out!"

?

MAD LIBS JUNIOR™ is fun to play with friends, but you can also play it by yourself! To begin, look at the story on the page below. When you come to a blank space in the story, look at the symbol that appears underneath. Then find the same symbol on this page and pick a word that appears below the symbol. Put that word in the blank space, and cross out the word, so you don't use it again. Continue doing this throughout the story until you've filled in all the spaces. Finally, read your story aloud and laugh!

DAZZLING DAPHNE

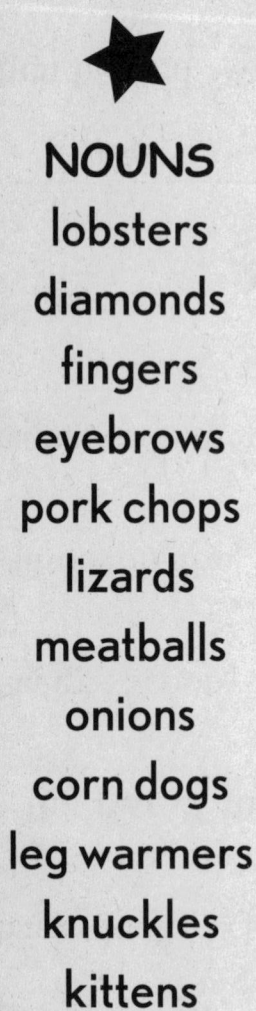

★ NOUNS	☺ ADJECTIVES	→ VERBS	? MISC.
lobsters	disgusting	giggle	ranch
diamonds	greasy	munch	concert
fingers	brainy	nibble	rest stop
eyebrows	bashful	sip	pet store
pork chops	chewy	sparkle	garden
lizards	creepy	sniff	bathroom
meatballs	dizzy	twist	attic
onions	dreamy	pinch	tree house
corn dogs	gross	kiss	jungle
leg warmers	grimy	smack	restaurant
knuckles	cheesy	poke	factory
kittens	scruffy	doodle	mall

Daphne was so _____! She couldn't wait for the dance at the

_____! To prepare for the _____ event, she went

shopping at her favorite store at the _____ called Sweet

_____. She bought a _____ purple dress, a pair

of _____ high-heeled _____, and some

_____ to tie in her hair. When she was done getting ready,

she looked _____! "Row, Raphne!" said Scooby. "Roo rook

_____." "Thanks, Scoob," replied Daphne. "You're so

_____. Would you like to _____ with me at the

dance?" "Rippee!" cried Scooby. "Rof rourse!" He put on a pair of stylish

_____ and grabbed Daphne's _____. "Ret's ro!"

exclaimed Scooby.

MAD LIBS JUNIOR™ is fun to play with friends, but you can also play it by yourself! To begin, look at the story on the page below. When you come to a blank space in the story, look at the symbol that appears underneath. Then find the same symbol on this page and pick a word that appears below the symbol. Put that word in the blank space, and cross out the word, so you don't use it again. Continue doing this throughout the story until you've filled in all the spaces. Finally, read your story aloud and laugh!

A DAY IN THE LIFE OF SCOOBY-DOO

★ NOUNS	☺ ADJECTIVES	→ VERBS	? MISC.
bubbles	scary	wiggles	airport
toilets	mushy	twirls	library
pickles	crunchy	chatters	cafeteria
diapers	giant	curls	fish tank
marshmallows	dizzy	kisses	barn
hot dogs	gooey	flips	stadium
eggs	slippery	showers	rodeo
lizards	chunky	zips	pigpen
tacos	grumpy	flaps	igloo
termites	chewy	cooks	pizzeria
roosters	squiggly	squeezes	arcade
clowns	cute	boogies	forest

Scooby is one busy dog! When he wakes up he _____ his bed ➡

and washes the _____. ★ Then he heads down to the

_____ ? to eat a big breakfast. Usually, he _____ ➡ a

big omelet made with _____ ★ and _____ ★ .Then he

usually _____ ➡ in the Mystery Machine with Shaggy and takes

a ride to the _____ ? to play their favorite video game, "Scary

_____ ★ ." Then they head to the _____ ? to hang out

with the rest of the gang. If Scooby and the gang aren't too busy solving

mysteries, they like to watch _____ ★ in the _____ ? .

Afterward, they head back to their _____ ? to go to sleep. Of

course, Shaggy always gives Scooby a few _____ Scooby

Snacks before bed. Night, night, Scooby!

MAD LIBS JUNIOR™ is fun to play with friends, but you can also play it by yourself! To begin, look at the story on the page below. When you come to a blank space in the story, look at the symbol that appears underneath. Then find the same symbol on this page and pick a word that appears below the symbol. Put that word in the blank space, and cross out the word, so you don't use it again. Continue doing this throughout the story until you've filled in all the spaces. Finally, read your story aloud and laugh!

BEST BUDS

★	☺	→	?
NOUNS	**ADJECTIVES**	**VERBS**	**MISC.**
french fries	creepy	drives	farm
tuna	yummy	flies	disco
elbows	salty	gives	tree house
sharks	sweet	wags	pizzeria
fingernails	furry	meows	deli
butterflies	soft	shouts	ocean
salmon	buttery	cooks	pet store
sneakers	spiky	twists	bathroom
twins	moist	swims	attic
knee socks	scary	shimmies	fish tank
puppies	wacky	laughs	ski lodge
beans	funny	smells	oven

BEST BUDS

There are no two _____ closer than Scooby and Shaggy. They

are inseparable! Shaggy _____ Scooby everywhere—to the

_____, the grocery store to buy _____, the

Laundromat to wash his dirty _____, and even his favorite

restaurant, the Tasty _____! Shaggy takes really good care of

Scooby. He gives Scooby a bath once a week so Scooby's coat will stay

nice and _____, and then he _____ him dry with

big, fluffy _____. After Scooby's _____ bath,

they'll either play a game of fetch in the _____, watch

_____ on their big-screen TV, or sit down in the

_____ and snack on _____. Shaggy can't

imagine life without Scooby!

MAD LIBS JUNIOR™ is fun to play with friends, but you can also play it by yourself! To begin, look at the story on the page below. When you come to a blank space in the story, look at the symbol that appears underneath. Then find the same symbol on this page and pick a word that appears below the symbol. Put that word in the blank space, and cross out the word, so you don't use it again. Continue doing this throughout the story until you've filled in all the spaces. Finally, read your story aloud and laugh!

A VICTORY FOR VELMA

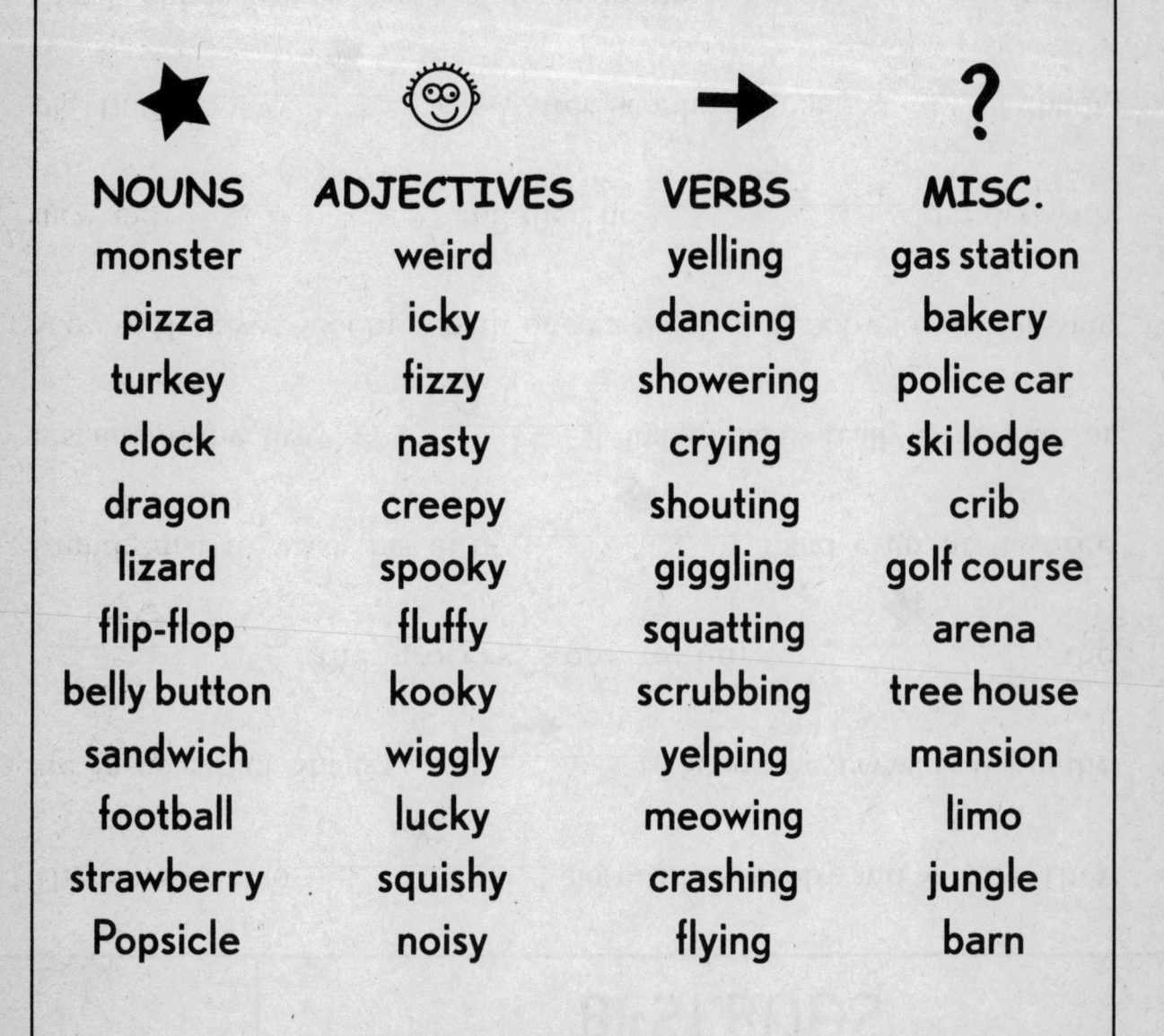

★ NOUNS	☺ ADJECTIVES	→ VERBS	? MISC.
monster	weird	yelling	gas station
pizza	icky	dancing	bakery
turkey	fizzy	showering	police car
clock	nasty	crying	ski lodge
dragon	creepy	shouting	crib
lizard	spooky	giggling	golf course
flip-flop	fluffy	squatting	arena
belly button	kooky	scrubbing	tree house
sandwich	wiggly	yelping	mansion
football	lucky	meowing	limo
strawberry	squishy	crashing	jungle
Popsicle	noisy	flying	barn

A VICTORY FOR VELMA

The Mystery Inc. gang was trying to solve their latest mystery. This time,

a/an _____ ☺ _____ ★ was on the loose! Suddenly,

Velma exclaimed, "Hey! Why don't we go down to the _____ ?

and see if a _____ ★ has seen anything suspicious!" When

Mystery Inc. arrived, they started to talk to all of the _____ ☺

people who were _____ ➡ in the _____ ? . One

person in particular was acting extremely _____ ☺ .Velma snuck

up behind him and grabbed a piece of his _____ ★ .When she

took it back to the _____ ? to test it, she found out it belonged

to Mr. Smithers from the _____ ? , who was wanted for stealing

a _____ ★ !

MAD LIBS JUNIOR™ is fun to play with friends, but you can also play it by yourself! To begin, look at the story on the page below. When you come to a blank space in the story, look at the symbol that appears underneath. Then find the same symbol on this page and pick a word that appears below the symbol. Put that word in the blank space, and cross out the word, so you don't use it again. Continue doing this throughout the story until you've filled in all the spaces. Finally, read your story aloud and laugh!

SCOOBY-DOO, WHERE ARE YOU?

★	☺	➡	?
NOUNS	**ADJECTIVES**	**VERBS**	**MISC.**
banana	plump	swim	submarine
egg	snowy	belly dance	igloo
worm	scary	wiggle	jungle gym
basketball	chewy	hoot	aquarium
caterpillar	sticky	find	lily pad
pretzel	slimy	yell	outhouse
toaster	mushy	mash	stable
sneaker	tired	squash	dining room
crayon	bubbly	bring	toilet bowl
TV	giggly	count	closet
handbag	creepy	smash	lake
peach	wacky	hide	taxi

One _____ day, the gang decided to _____ → over to

the _____ ? to play a game of _____ → -and-seek. "Okay,

Scoob," said Shaggy. "You go first. Count to ten and then come and

_____ → for us." "Rokay," replied Scooby. He closed his

_____ ★ and counted to ten. "Rook rout, rere ri rome!" cried

Scooby. He ran to the _____ ? and looked under the

_____ ★. Sure enough, there were Fred and Daphne! Then he

checked high up in the _____ ? and found Velma. But he

couldn't _____ → Shaggy anywhere! He looked under

the _____ ? and even in the _____ ?. Then Scooby had an

idea. He ran over and opened the _____ ★ and there was Shaggy!

"_____ job, Scoob!" said Shaggy. "You deserve a Scooby Snack!"

MAD LIBS JUNIOR™ is fun to play with friends, but you can also play it by yourself! To begin, look at the story on the page below. When you come to a blank space in the story, look at the symbol that appears underneath. Then find the same symbol on this page and pick a word that appears below the symbol. Put that word in the blank space, and cross out the word, so you don't use it again. Continue doing this throughout the story until you've filled in all the spaces. Finally, read your story aloud and laugh!

A CLUE FOR SCOOBY-DOO, PART IV

★	😊	➡	?
NOUNS	**ADJECTIVES**	**VERBS**	**MISC.**
hamburger	tired	crept	backyard
cookie	crazy	flew	kitchen
toilet	kooky	washed	aquarium
goldfish	sweet	blew	dollhouse
dog	rough	squashed	post office
milkshake	scaly	twisted	cabin
diamond	lovely	cried	pet store
computer	gross	yelled	garden
clam	crunchy	turned	bakery
dragon	creepy	boogied	library
caterpillar	sticky	screamed	stadium
bagel	icy	sniffed	Dumpster

The gang and the museum owner hopped in the Mystery Machine

and drove to the _____ **?** to talk to the possible thief. When

they arrived, they found the _____ **?** totally empty. Fred

_____ **➡** around and said, "Maybe he went to the _____. **?**

Let's catch him before his _____ **★** takes off!" The gang quickly

_____ **➡** to the airport and sure enough there was the thief! "I

can't believe that you would steal my _____ **★**!" yelled the

museum owner. "Give me back my _____ **★**!" The thief tried to

run away, but then a police _____ **★** showed up and

_____ **➡** him. After the thief _____ **➡** with the police to

go to the _____ **?**, Shaggy gave Scooby a Scooby Snack!

MAD LIBS JUNIOR™ is fun to play with friends, but you can also play it by yourself! To begin, look at the story on the page below. When you come to a blank space in the story, look at the symbol that appears underneath. Then find the same symbol on this page and pick a word that appears below the symbol. Put that word in the blank space, and cross out the word, so you don't use it again. Continue doing this throughout the story until you've filled in all the spaces. Finally, read your story aloud and laugh!

SPOOKY SURPRISES

★ NOUNS	☺ ADJECTIVES	➡ VERBS	? MISC.
ghosts	brave	smash	kitchen
frogs	cute	meow	toilet
gorillas	scary	paddle	roller rink
chickens	cuddly	flop	sailboat
eyebrows	smelly	kick	arcade
garbage cans	nice	splash	barn
sardines	greasy	chew	bookstore
livers	bony	wash	cafe
nachos	wide	cry	island
tigers	tired	scatter	sauna
pancakes	cheery	zig	bakery
telephones	chubby	bounce	pigpen

MAD LIBS JUNIOR.
SPOOKY SURPRISES

One of the _____ things about being part of Mystery Inc. is that

the gang never knows what _____ surprises will come their

way! As detectives, they have to travel to _____ places

like the _____ and the _____ to find spooky

_____ and ghouly _____. One time when Scooby

and the gang went to a _____ amusement park, they couldn't

believe all the _____ that were waiting for them! As they

walked toward the _____, a spooky group of _____

went flying past them! Then a huge _____ vampire started to

_____ them! Another time when they had to investigate an

abandoned _____, they saw so many _____ that the

gang immediately started to _____!

MAD LIBS JUNIOR™ is fun to play with friends, but you can also play it by yourself! To begin, look at the story on the page below. When you come to a blank space in the story, look at the symbol that appears underneath. Then find the same symbol on this page and pick a word that appears below the symbol. Put that word in the blank space, and cross out the word, so you don't use it again. Continue doing this throughout the story until you've filled in all the spaces. Finally, read your story aloud and laugh!

SCOOBY SNACKS

★	☺	➜	?
NOUNS	**ADJECTIVES**	**VERBS**	**MISC.**
apples	fruity	wag	ballet
frogs	rotten	wrap	stadium
hot dogs	steamy	blend	birdhouse
pickles	yummy	mush	litter box
bathtubs	sweaty	bark	zoo
waffles	disgusting	glide	campsite
ears	slimy	pucker	ski lodge
potatoes	moldy	bounce	beach
noodles	juicy	fly	bakery
puppies	furry	scream	cafeteria
carrots	happy	scribble	gym
marshmallows	sugary	chomp	garage

If there is one thing that Scooby loves to do, it's eat! For breakfast, he and

Shaggy usually _____ ➡ in the Mystery Machine and drive

to the _____ ❓, where they order yummy _____ ★.

For lunch, Scooby's favorite meal is _____ 😊 pizza topped with

crunchy _____ ★ and extra _____ ★. Sometimes,

when Scooby is extra _____ 😊, Mystery Inc. will surprise him

and _____ ➡ him to his favorite ice-cream parlor, where Scooby

and Shaggy share a _____ 😊 sundae called the Giant

_____ ❓. It's _____ 😊! It's three scoops of vanilla

_____ ★ topped with chocolate _____ ★, peanut

butter _____ ★, and _____ 😊 cherries. Yum!

MAD LIBS JUNIOR™ is fun to play with friends, but you can also play it by yourself! To begin, look at the story on the page below. When you come to a blank space in the story, look at the symbol that appears underneath. Then find the same symbol on this page and pick a word that appears below the symbol. Put that word in the blank space, and cross out the word, so you don't use it again. Continue doing this throughout the story until you've filled in all the spaces. Finally, read your story aloud and laugh!

FOLLOW THE LEADER

★ NOUNS	☺ ADJECTIVES	➡ VERBS	? MISC.
hair	tired	whisper	office
hot dogs	happy	crawl	festival
cream puffs	loopy	slap	restaurant
trampolines	smart	shimmy	zoo
socks	goofy	boogie	jungle
toenails	quirky	wag	toy store
onions	sneaky	prowl	bathroom
flip-flops	loony	giggle	mall
oranges	smiley	try	beach
pizzas	slimy	waddle	pizzeria
puppies	grubby	jiggle	deli
peanuts	skinny	jump	toilet

Fred is the leader of Mystery Inc. He is a really _____ detective!

As the group leader, he makes sure he always looks _____. His

trademark outfit is a _____ white sweater, a red T-shirt, and blue

_____. Every time the gang finds out about a _____

disappearance of _____ in the _____, Fred can't wait

to _____ on the case! And he always gets to _____

in the Mystery Machine! With the help of _____ Daphne,

brainy Velma, _____ Shaggy and his _____ sidekick

Scooby, Fred can _____ any _____ that come his

way! Like Fred always says, "Well, that wraps up this mystery!"

MAD LIBS JUNIOR™ is fun to play with friends, but you can also play it by yourself! To begin, look at the story on the page below. When you come to a blank space in the story, look at the symbol that appears underneath. Then find the same symbol on this page and pick a word that appears below the symbol. Put that word in the blank space, and cross out the word, so you don't use it again. Continue doing this throughout the story until you've filled in all the spaces. Finally, read your story aloud and laugh!

THE HAUNTED AMUSEMENT PARK

★ NOUNS	☺ ADJECTIVES	➡ VERBS	? MISC.
porcupine	wild	march	stable
milkshake	spooky	run	desert
pretzel	slippery	beg	jungle
onion	dirty	bark	warehouse
salmon	stinky	play	Dumpster
radio	gooey	chop	bathtub
wart	scary	sway	roller rink
pizza	sleepy	swim	playground
caterpillar	crusty	paddle	pizzeria
shrimp	pretty	kick	doghouse
string bean	gross	waddle	classroom
roach	bubbly	jump	kitchen

THE HAUNTED AMUSEMENT PARK

One day the gang decided to go to the amusement park. Velma couldn't

wait to _____ ➡ on the Ferris _____ ★ , while Daphne

and Shaggy wanted to take a ride on the Zippity _____ ★ . But

suddenly Shaggy yelled, "Zoinks! This place looks _____ 😊 !" All

of the rides were closed, except for a _____ 😊 haunted house.

It was covered with _____ 😊 cobwebs, and there were eerie

sounds coming from the _____ ? . Suddenly, the gang spotted

_____ 😊 monsters that started to _____ ➡ after them!

"Rikes!" cried Scooby. "Ret's ro!"

MAD LIBS JUNIOR™ is fun to play with friends, but you can also play it by yourself! To begin, look at the story on the page below. When you come to a blank space in the story, look at the symbol that appears underneath. Then find the same symbol on this page and pick a word that appears below the symbol. Put that word in the blank space, and cross out the word, so you don't use it again. Continue doing this throughout the story until you've filled in all the spaces. Finally, read your story aloud and laugh!

SCOOBY AND FRIENDS

NOUNS	**ADJECTIVES**	**VERBS**	**MISC.**
tadpoles	juicy	shout	concert
chimps	fresh	smile	pizzeria
cookies	silly	waddle	museum
balloons	smart	bop	mall
horses	giggly	smack	zoo
brussels sprouts	sleepy	hop	diner
tacos	jumpy	boogie	park
parents	nasty	flip	deli
toilets	gross	zip	bakery
kittens	squishy	scramble	doghouse
french fries	wiggly	mix	stadium
clams	creepy	leap	golf course

MAD LIBS JUNIOR
SCOOBY AND FRIENDS

Scooby is probably the most _____ dog ever! He always has

_____ to help him and Mystery Inc. do their detective work!

Every weekend, his friends Scooby Dum and Scooby Dee come to

_____ with the gang. They are so _____! Whenever

they come to visit, Scooby can't help but _____. And they love

to eat crunchy _____ more than Scooby does! And can you

believe that celebrities come to the _____ to visit the gang?

One time, the Three _____ came! They were so

_____ that the gang couldn't stop laughing! Another time, the

sports team the Harlem _____ came to _____! They

taught Scooby and Shaggy how to _____ hoops in the

_____!

MAD LIBS JUNIOR™ is fun to play with friends, but you can also play it by yourself! To begin, look at the story on the page below. When you come to a blank space in the story, look at the symbol that appears underneath. Then find the same symbol on this page and pick a word that appears below the symbol. Put that word in the blank space, and cross out the word, so you don't use it again. Continue doing this throughout the story until you've filled in all the spaces. Finally, read your story aloud and laugh!

BON VOYAGE!

★ NOUNS	☺ ADJECTIVES	➡ VERBS	? MISC.
ghosts	scary	hooted	rodeo
skateboards	whiny	boogied	garden
bagels	sweet	zipped	toy store
peppers	yucky	flapped	golf course
chickens	quiet	grinned	bathroom
tomatoes	smelly	shimmied	castle
lollipops	crispy	chattered	farm
monkeys	puffy	flipped	restaurant
eyebrows	cool	boiled	bakery
tails	mushy	cracked	classroom
jeans	gassy	spooked	fish tank
peas	meaty	ate	barn

BON VOYAGE!

After Scooby and the gang solved the Mystery of the Haunted

_____, they decided to take a vacation. They _____ ➡

in the Mystery Machine and _____ ➡ to a _____ beach

town in the _____ ? . When they arrived, they spent the first few

hours at the _____ ? , eating _____ and talking about

_____ . But suddenly the gang started to hear weird

_____ and see _____ shadows. Suddenly, Velma

screamed, "Look! I just saw a group of _____ villains jump into

the _____ ? !" The gang quickly left the _____ ? and

_____ ➡ to the van. "Rut, roh," cried Scooby. "Don't worry, Scoob,"

assured Fred. "We'll get the scary _____ ." So much for a

_____ vacation!